GUARDIAN ANGEL
Rescue on the Glacier

By Jesse Peterson

Illustrated by Manuela Soriani

Text © 2013 Jesse Peterson
Illustrations © 2013 Manuela Soriani & Jesse Peterson
Typesetting & pre-print by Mattia Bulgarelli
All rights reserved.

Rescue Me Publishing, LLC.

ISBN 978-0-9885950-8-8

No portion of this book may be copied or reproduced without written consent from the author or illustrator.

To contact either one, please visit *www.guardianangelrescues.com*

For Cadence,
and others who dream big.
Never quit!

As the plane took off, leaving the runway behind, Benny and Jill pressed their noses against the glass windows next to their seats. They watched as the ground fell away beneath them.

Up and up into the sky they went, as the little plane turned and headed towards the steep mountain range on the edge of town.

Benny and his family lived in Texas and this was their first visit to Alaska. As a special treat, the children's parents had arranged for them to view the Knik Glacier from the air.

The gigantic mountain covered in ice and snow was not far from the city of Anchorage, and on this warm summer morning the view was sure to be fantastic.

As they flew closer and closer to the glacier, the mountains looked bigger and bigger. "Hey Benny, check out those clouds over there!" Jill said excitedly, pointing to a bank of clouds that seemed to have appeared out of nowhere. Benny turned his head to see what his sister was talking about.

As he looked, the wall of puffy clouds ahead of them seemed to be racing towards them. In seconds, the mountains disappeared into whiteness.

The plane shook a little from side to side, blown around by the wind. Snow tapped against the windows. "I'm sorry about this folks," Don the pilot said. "I've never seen weather move in this fast." Benny could hardly believe what he was seeing. It was summer! How could it be snowing? His little sister grabbed his hand and squeezed it tight. Usually, Benny would have told her to cut it out, but he could see that she was scared. He was scared too, so he tightened his grip on her hand.

After fighting the storm for what felt like hours, Don decided that they would be better off landing. "Our best bet is for me to land on the glacier," Don said. "There is snow on the surface and it is kinda flat, so I should be able to put her down okay." He started to ease the plane down. How can he know where the ground is, Benny wondered? After all, Don couldn't see anything but white cloud outside the windshield. Benny and Jill held hands even tighter as the plane rocked and bucked.

All of a sudden, there was a horrible bump. The plane skipped across the surface of the glacier like a stone across a pond.

They heard a loud screeching and tearing noise. Benny and his sister held each other tight.

At last the plane stopped moving. The pilot, who had smacked his nose on the windshield, turned to talk to the passengers. "I'm fine folks, and it looks like my nose was the only casualty," he said, trying to be cheerful. He went outside to check the damage. As he opened the door, the wind whipped at his face and he sank deep into the snow. His pants were soaked with snow and ice after just a few steps. Before long he scurried back inside the airplane, his cheeks bright red.

"The good news is that the plane is basically in one piece and it will protect us from the storm. The bad news is that we have no food, no water, and no winter clothes. We are going to need help, and soon," Don told his passengers. Next, Don set off the emergency transmitter and started talking into the radio. Benny looked out of the window at the storm and wondered if someone out there would hear the message. How long could they survive huddled together inside the plane? It was freezing cold, and the blowing snow was starting to bury their little plane.

Back in Anchorage, at the Rescue Coordination Center, an alarm went off. Bailey ran over to a computer to find out where the signal was coming from. As he stared at the screen, a radio started squawking. A pilot told Bailey that he had just talked to Don, and that Don's plane had gone down on the glacier. "He has four passengers and no supplies. They need help now," the pilot said. Quickly, Bailey phoned the on-call rescue team. This sounded like a job for the Guardian Angels, commonly known as Pararescuemen or PJs.

Jesse, brand new to the rescue team, was playing with his daughter in their backyard when his work phone rang. He knew that this call could only mean one thing; someone was in trouble. This would be his first Alaska rescue mission. He listened closely to what Bailey said, kissed his daughter goodbye, and in just a few minutes he was in his car racing to the military base.

The Guardian Angel team members met at the base, and they quickly assembled their gear for the rescue. Soon the four of them: Jesse, Angel, Al, and Chris were in the back of a helicopter flying at full speed towards the glacier. "This should be a routine job guys," the experienced crew determined. "If we can land up there, we should be able to pick everyone up and make it home in time for dinner with our families."

When they got to the crash site high on the mountain, everyone looked down and realized that this was not going to be a simple rescue. The two pilots could hardly see a thing through the blowing snow. They tried to land the helicopter, but it was just too dangerous. When the team tried to drop supplies to the survivors below, gale force winds blew the packs full of warm clothes and blankets down the mountain. "It looks like we are going to have to land lower on the glacier, underneath the storm, and ski up through the blizzard to get to them," Al said. So much for getting home soon, they all thought.

Soon, the team members were near the base of the glacier unloading their equipment from the helicopter onto the snowy ground. Daylight was fading as the storm raged higher on the mountain.

The surface of the glacier was not smooth. Instead, there were hundreds of deep crevasses everywhere. Just in case someone fell into one of those bottomless cracks in the ice, the members of the team roped themselves together for safety; Jesse to Chris and Angel to Al. Next, the men put on their skis, hitched themselves to sleds loaded with supplies, and started skiing up the mountain towards the crashed airplane. The rescue pilots wished them well and flew away, leaving the team alone as they trekked upwards towards the storm.

Before long, they entered the blizzard. A wall of freezing wind and snow blasted the men. Jesse pulled his hat down over his ears and zipped up his jacket as high as possible, right up to his chin. *Brrrrrrrr*, he thought to himself. The snow was blowing so hard that the men couldn't see past the tips of their skis.

Carefully navigating around all the crevasses, the team was forced to take it slow. The howling wind knocked them over every now and then, but each time they got back up and continued climbing towards the family in distress.

Though all four men were strong and very fit, they found skiing up the glacier under those conditions exhausting. Knowing that the people in the plane were counting on them, they skied up the mountain until they had no energy left. They were going to have to rest for a bit. It was early in the morning and they had been climbing upwards all night without a break. The temperature was falling fast.

Quickly the four men dug a deep hole in the snow and they put up a tent in the sheltered space. Angel melted some snow in a titanium pot using a tiny camp stove, and soon the guys were sipping on water. This warmed them up a bit and would help prevent dehydration. They shared some trail mix, which gave their bodies precious energy. No one said much as they ate, drank and stretched their cramping legs. Their thoughts were on the people in need, higher on the mountain.

When the sun began to rise, the team was on the move again. Skiing up the glacier was going so slowly that Jesse decided to try walking on the snow; perhaps this would be easier for the guys. He removed his heavy skis and took one step. His legs sank into the snow up to his thighs. Gritting his teeth, he said, "No luck boys!" He put his skis back on and the team continued climbing.

After hours and hours of traveling, the men found themselves facing a new problem. Ahead of them there was a wide crevasse and above the only path was a cornice, a towering overhang of ice and snow. The cornice was the size of a gigantic house and it was perched on the side of the mountain. The team knew cornices were dangerously unstable, but they also knew that farther up the mountain five people were depending on them.

Carefully, Jesse, Angel, Al, and Chris skirted their way along the edge of the crevasse under the overhang, hoping and praying that the snow and ice above them would hold together. They knew that at any moment the cornice could collapse, and they would be buried in an instant. Ever so carefully they moved forward.

Finally, the four men reached the plane's coordinates, but there was nothing there! The team decided they should split up to increase their chances of finding the plane and its passengers. Jesse and Chris went right, and Angel and Al continued up the glacier.

Just as the sun was slipping behind the mountain for the second night, Benny saw shadowy figures appear out of nowhere. For a few seconds he forgot to breathe, and he quickly reached for his sister's hand. Then, when the figures got closer, he realized that there were two rescuers out there and not a pair of snow monsters.

"They're here to save us!" Benny yelled excitedly. The people inside the plane were incredibly relieved, and they gave Jesse and Chris an enthusiastic welcome. Though they were cold, exhausted and frostbitten, the two men got to work. First, they gave the passengers warm clothes and blankets. This is better than Christmas, thought Benny as he slipped a jacket over his head. The rescuers put up a tent under the wing of the plane and melted snow until they had enough warm water for the passengers to drink. As midnight approached, Jesse and Chris settled into their tent to warm up, but they couldn't relax. They thought about their teammates, who were still somewhere on the glacier searching in the blizzard. With the blizzard in full force outside, it was impossible to guide them in. Nobody slept a wink.

Finally, early the next morning, Angel and Al found the crash site. Relieved, Jesse and Chris ran out to meet them. Another tent was set up for the two men so that they could escape from the freezing weather.

Al retrieved the satellite phone from their sled and the team made a call back to base headquarters. Unfortunately, there had been another emergency several hundred miles away, and the Air Force had sent all of their helicopters to help. Bailey, back at the Rescue Coordination Center, called around to locate someone else who could fly up the glacier to pick everyone up. As the weather was improving slightly, Bailey arranged for an Army helicopter to assist as soon as possible.

Everyone was thrilled when they heard the sound of a helicopter later that afternoon. At long last they were going to get off the frigid glacier! The aircraft appeared out of the whiteness, and Benny and his family cheered with excitement. Just as it was about to land, the Army helicopter tipped and its rotor blades smacked the surface of the glacier. Pieces of metal broke off and flew through the air in every direction. The helicopter crashed right in front of them, rolling a few times before it lay still.

The Guardian Angel team ran towards the helicopter to help, praying that everyone was okay. Though the three soldiers on board were shaken up, by some miracle they weren't injured. The rescue team looked them over, then pitched another tent for them. Shivering, they said "thanks" as they climbed inside the tent to warm themselves. The little camp on the glacier was growing!

Finally, at around sundown later that day, an Air Force rescue helicopter arrived on the scene. Conditions were still poor, and the helicopter could only carry three people on board for the trip down the glacier. It was decided that Benny, Jill, and their mother would go first. The Guardian Angel team, the Army men, Don the pilot, and Benny's father stayed another night on the glacier before they were picked up at around noon the next day.

When Benny and his family were reunited with the Guardian Angel team back in Anchorage, there was a lot of hugging, backslapping, and handshaking. Everyone was in good spirits after their unexpected adventure on the glacier.

With tears in her eyes, Benny's mom thanked each of the men for risking their lives. "Our pleasure Ma'am," they said. "We would do it all over again in a heartbeat."

After all the hugs and excitement was over, the team gathered their equipment and hopped back onto the helicopter for the short flight back to the Air Force Base. As they lifted off from the ground, a wonderful feeling swept over the men. They had done their job well and could finally relax.

Jesse closed his eyes and smiled. He thought of his beautiful daughter, who was at home and waiting anxiously to jump into his arms when he walked through the door. Everyone involved in the mission had reason to smile; they had represented the community to the best of their ability, and lived up to their rescue motto:

"**These Things We Do, That Others May Live.**"

Believe it or not, this is based on a true story.

Every year numerous small planes across the country are forced to have emergency landings. This particular Guardian Angel team, made up of three Pararescuemen (Angel, Al and Chris) and one Combat Rescue Officer (Jesse), took on considerable risk while climbing up the glacier because they believed the family huddled inside the airplane wouldn't survive the freezing temperatures brought on by the blizzard. Although each of them were hypothermic and frostbitten by the time they reached the crash site, they would jump at the chance to do it all over again.

For more information on how to become a Guardian Angel team member, or for more details on the actual Knik Glacier rescue, visit the following websites:

"The Forgotten Rescue." *Alaska Dispatch.* January 7, 2011.
http://www.alaskadispatch.com/article/forgotten-rescue-recounting-knik-glacier-crash

"Pilots Three-Day Wait For Rescue Off Glacier." *All Things Considered.*
National Public Radio (NPR). August 13, 2010.
http://www.npr.org/templates/story/story.php?storyId=129183537

"Guardian Angel - Rescue on the Glacier." *Rescue Me Publishing, LLC.*
http://www.guardianangelrescues.com

"Volume VII." *Portraits in Courage.* US Air Force. 2012.
http://www.af.mil/specials/courage/07uriarte.html

"Guardian Angel." *Air Combat Command.* US Air Force.
http://www.acc.af.mil/library/guardianangel.asp

Warning!

No one should attempt glacier travel, or camping in blizzard conditions, without adult supervision.

Proper training and quality mountaineering equipment is a must.

This Guardian Angel team was outfitted with some of the world's finest equipment, yet they still had to fight for survival at times while performing this rescue.

Are you up for a challenge?

See how many hidden helicopters you can find throughout the book!

What is a Guardian Angel?

Guardian Angel team members are some of the most elite, highly trained members in the United States military. Their mission is to "save life and aid the injured."

Once Guardian Angel team members make it through a very challenging initial selection course, called INDOC, they are trained in emergency medicine, taught how to parachute from airplanes, climb up mountains, scuba dive and to survive in any situation.

They do whatever it takes to help someone who is in trouble. If they get knocked down, they always get back up.

When times get tough, they smile and look forward to conquering the challenge. They are "quiet professionals" and they have some truly amazing stories to share.

Pararescue (PJ)
Combat Rescue Officer (CRO)
Survival, Evasion, Resistance, Escape (SERE)

Author's note

I wish to acknowledge and thank my family, friends and teammates who have helped with this rewarding project. It began as a make-believe book for my daughter over three years ago, with a superhero rescue dog as the main character. Since then it has morphed into this final nonfiction version, in order to share the real story as accurately as possible.

This book recounts the rescue mission as perceived through our team's experience and the illustrator's imagination. Some characters have been changed in lieu of privacy. Some images and events were simply too complex to portray in this medium.

There were literally hundreds of rescue professionals working behind the scenes to ensure success throughout this multi-day mission. Thousands more, all around the world, are out there demonstrating "service before self" day after day. The rescue community is truly one of a kind; talented, motivated and selfless! May this book serve as a small tribute to the sacrifices they continually make.

Illustrator's note

First of all, I wish to thank Jesse for being such a pleasant personality to work with throughout this long process. From the very start of the project, I always felt his passion to represent the rescue community as accurately as possible. It was nice to work with such a supportive person, always encouraging and willing to provide extra guidance so that my illustrations could be as precise as possible.

I'm excited that our work may help others understand the importance of teamwork, physical fitness and never giving up. It's reassuring to think that there are people all over the world, from my country of Italy all the way to the United States, who are willing to push their physical and mental limits to aid people in sticky situations.

As I read through this, I have to remind myself that these guys are not just make believe, fictional characters; they really do exist! I wish the best of luck to the entire rescue community; always training for the worst-case scenario and working hard for our safety.

Made in the USA
San Bernardino, CA
28 February 2014